The Perfect Siesta

Pato Mena

It was the middle of the day in the jungle and the **jaguar** was very **hot.**

All of a sudden a **cool breeze** started to blow and the big cat thought,

"Roar! What a nice breeze. It would be perfect to take a siesta."

Just then the jaguar saw a **coati**
sitting on a branch up in a tree,
and he said,

"Hey! Could you do me a big favor? I have something really **important** to do, but first I would like to take a little **siesta.** There's such a nice, cool breeze. It's just too good to resist!

Could you wake me up in exactly **10 minutes**?"

"**Of course**, Mr. Jaguar," answered the scared coati.

"You go right ahead and take your nice siesta. **I'll wake you up**."

And just like that, the jaguar dropped off into a **deep sleep**.

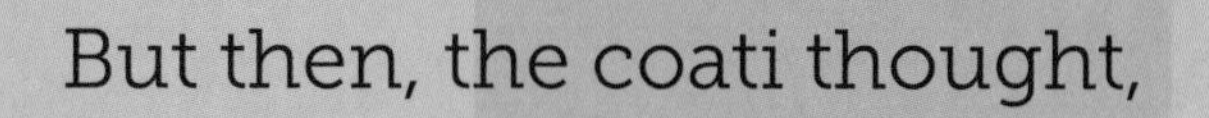

But then, the coati thought,

"Hmm... it's true. It would be a shame not to take advantage of this pleasant breeze."

So the coati said to a **cockatiel,** who was perched just a few branches above,

"Hey! Could you do me a **favor**? I have to wake the jaguar up in 10 minutes because he has something very, very important to do, but first I want to take a **little siesta**.
There is such a nice, cool breeze. It's just too good to resist!

Would you mind waking me up in **10 minutes**?"

"Of course!" said the kind cockatiel.

"Go ahead and take your siesta. **I'll wake you up**."

And just like that, the coati dropped off into a **deep sleep**.

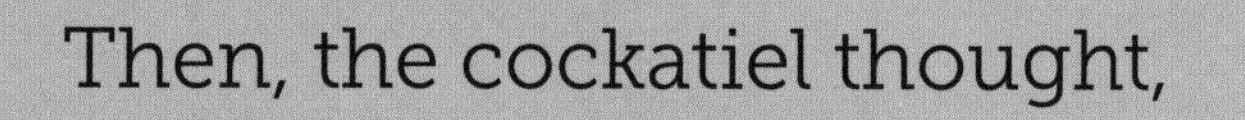

Then, the cockatiel thought,

"Hmm... There's no denying it.
That really is a pleasant breeze."

So he said to the only
animal that was close by,

"Hey! You there! **Sloth!** I have to wake up the **coati** who has to wake up the **jaguar** who has something very, very important to do. But first, I would like to take a siesta.
There is such a nice, cool breeze. It's just too good to resist!

Would you be so kind as to wake me up in exactly **10 minutes**?"

"Really? Why?
Sure... Uh...
of course! What?"
replied the sleepy sloth.

"Wake me up! In exactly
10 minutes," repeated the cockatiel.

"It's very **important**.
You have to stay awake!"

"Zzzzzzsure... zzzzzsure... ten minutes... no worriezzzz..." said the sloth with a big yawn.

"Thank you so much!" said the cockatiel, who dropped off into a deep sleep.

Just then, the sloth felt the **cool breeze** and realized that she should ask some other animal to wake her up in **10 minutes**, but...

there was no one awake to ask!

This was such **torture** for the poor **sloth!**
But she had given her word to the **cockatiel,**
who had promised the **coati,**
who had promised the **jaguar,**
(who, no one was particularly thrilled to see **angry**).

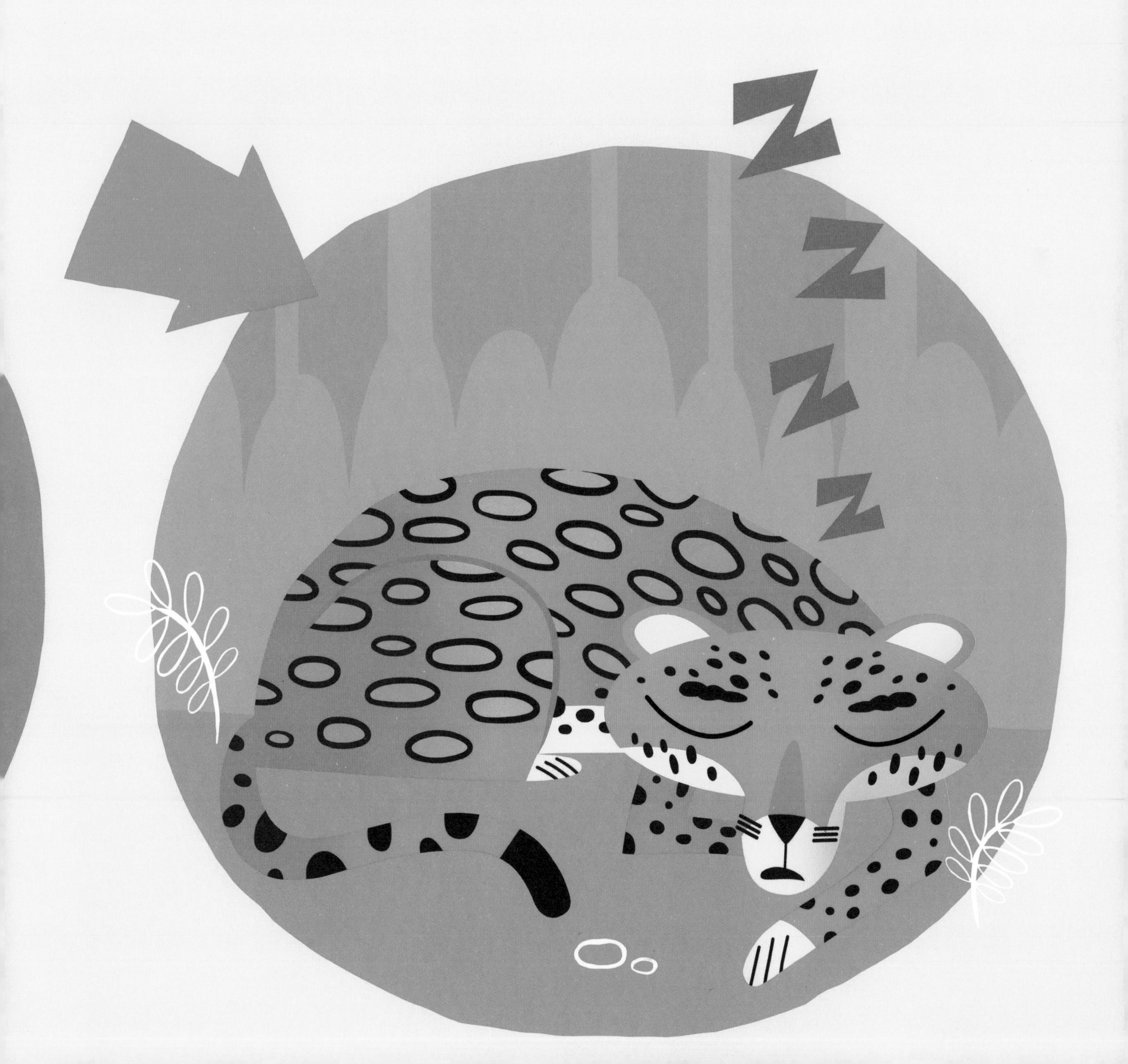

"I have got to stay awake," she said to herself.

One, two, three minutes went by.
The sloth was **battling sleep** more
than any other sloth in **sloth history.**

Four, five, **six** more minutes went by.

She could almost hear the breeze whisper:

Seven, eight, nine
more minutes went by.

Her **eyelids**
got heavier and **heavier**...

And just when there was only **one more minute** left before she had to wake the cockatiel up,

The sloth fell fast asleep...

ZZZZZZZZ

Then, all of a sudden, the nice, **cool breeze** that was blowing through the jungle turned into a **huge...**

ZZZZZHHHHNN

NGGG...

The **tremendously loud snore** of the **sloth** woke up

the cockatiel, the coati, and the jaguar...

Bang! Right on the **tenth minute!**

ZZZHNG